DAVID'S
LITTLE INDIAN

A Story by Margaret Wise Brown

Illustrated by Remy Charlip

A YOUNG YEARLING BOOK

Published by
Dell Publishing
a division of
Bantam Doubleday Dell Publishing Group, Inc.
666 Fifth Avenue
New York, New York 10103

Reprinted by arrangement with WaterMark, Inc.
Printed in the United States of America

February 1992

10 9 8 7 6 5 4 3 2 1

WES

DAVID'S LITTLE INDIAN

Once upon a time, and in a time we are now living, a little boy, deep in the deepest woods, found a very solemn and very small Indian. He was no bigger than an ear of corn. But no matter how small, he was a real Indian–even with feathers in his hair.

The little Indian was drowsily
leaning back against a rock looking
at the sky when the little boy found
him. And to make certain he was
real, the little boy pushed him. Then
the little boy asked him a question to
see if he would talk.

"What day is it?" asked the boy.

Now this was the right question,
for that was what the little Indian was
most interested in, and that is what
he had been thinking about as he
leaned against the rock.

"What day is it?" asked the little
boy again more softly.

The little Indian answered...

"DAY OF THE DARK BRIGHT LIGHT."

And the boy looked up and saw the dark bright light of that late summer day.

The distances were clear and nothing looked very far away.

"My name is David," said the boy.

"Carpe Diem," said the little Indian.

"What does it mean?" asked the boy, for he knew that all Indian names mean something.

"Carpe Diem means in your language 'Seize-the-Day,'" said the little Indian. *"It is a Latin name meaning 'Wo No So' in Indian. What does David mean?"*

"I don't know," said the boy.

"David must mean something," grunted the little Indian, and he gave a little shrug.

"What day was yesterday?" asked the boy.

And the little Indian said...

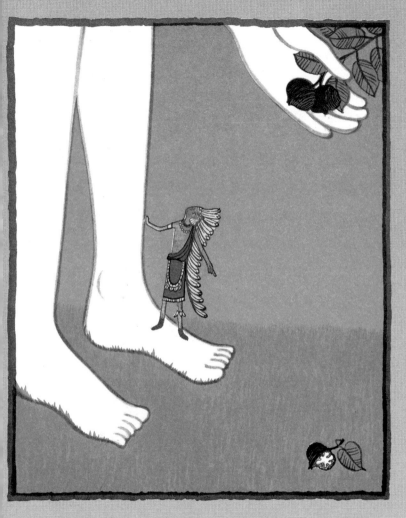

DAY OF THE FIRST NUT THAT FELL

The little Indian loved the days as they came and went, and he watched them. He never said much—mostly what day it was and a few grunts.

Of course, the little boy kept him with him always. Who wouldn't, if they found a little tiny friend in the woods for their very own!

Back in the world of tables and chairs and going places and grown-up people, no one noticed the little Indian with the boy, because no one expected to see a little Indian. But he was there all right.

And together they watched the days come and go, the boy and his Indian.

DAY OF THE BRIGHT GREEN TREE

DAY OF THE MOON IN THE DAY

DAY OF THE LITTLE BLUE DISH

DAY OF THE YELLOW LEAVES FALLING

DAY OF THE BIRDS FLYING AWAY

DAY OF THE UNEXPECTED SNOW

DAY OF THE COLD NOSE

THE DAY IT DIDN'T SNOW

AND THE DAY IT DID.

"What day was it the day before I first found you?" asked the boy.

THE DAY BEFORE I MET YOU

Nights and days went down the sky and it was spring.

DAY OF THE FIRST ROBIN

The boy and his Indian decided to become blood brothers, so they pricked their fingers and let their blood mingle together.

"Now what day it is for you is the day it is for me."

From then on they didn't have to talk together. Each almost knew what the other was thinking. All about them, grown-ups talked and talked and talked and talked and talked and talked.

"What day is it, Carpe?" asked the boy when at last they were alone that night.

DAY OF THE DREARY GROWN-UPS

And the next morning they went away into the woods, where there were no grown-ups.

DAY OF THE TALL COOL TREES

DAY OF THE FIRST TRILLIUM

DAY THE SUN FELT WARM

It was summer. And all summer
they lived in the woods. They built a
house of green branches and a bed of
pine needles, and they lived there
together.

DAY OF THE SMALL GREEN BOWER

DAY OF THE WHITE DAISIES

DAY OF THE BIG MOON COMING UP

Then, late one night, winter came
whistling in.

DAY OF THE CRYSTAL TREE

And they found a little cave and lined it with warm leaves and fur rugs.

And the winter passed.

DAY THE FIRE BURNED LIKE
FEATHERS SPEAKING

DAY OF THE DARK BRANCHES

DAY THE CROCUS BLOOMED

And it was spring again, so they made up a song.

It was a wonderful life, that life of the boy and his Indian. And they grew up and never missed a day.